The Bermuda Mystery

N. A. Seidel

Urban Tales

This book is dedicated to all the dreamers, explorers, and storytellers. With every page, we venture into the unknown—places where myths live, mysteries unravel, and the impossible becomes reality. These short stories are just the beginning of countless adventures that lie ahead. May this series ignite your imagination and take you to lands you've never seen before. Here's to many more tales that inspire, thrill, and transport us to worlds we've only dreamed of – N. A. Seidel

CONTENTS

Prologue

Urban Tales

ISBN: 978-1-7636920-4-6

PROLOGUE

THE DISAPPEARANCE OF FLIGHT 829

1972. Somewhere over the Bermuda Triangle.

The engines hummed steadily, a familiar rhythm that lulled the passengers of Flight 829 into a false sense of calm. Captain Reynolds checked his instruments for the third time in ten minutes, a frown etched deep on his face. Everything was fine—until it wasn't. "Captain, there's something wrong with the compass," came the voice of First Officer Harris. "It's spinning like crazy."

Reynolds leaned forward, eyes narrowing at the panel. The compass needle whipped around in erratic circles as if pulled by an unseen force. "That's impossible," he muttered, flicking switches and tapping dials. But every instrument he checked had gone haywire. The altimeter, the navigation system—everything was malfunctioning.

The co-pilot's voice grew tight with concern. "We're losing radar contact, sir." A low, vibrating hum filled the cockpit.

At first, it was barely noticeable, but soon, it grew louder, reverberating through the plane's metal frame. Reynolds' hands tightened around the controls as he scanned the horizon. A strange light—a glow—began forming in the distance. Unlike anything he had seen, an otherworldly shimmer pulsed in the darkening sky.

"Do you see that?" Harris asked, his voice tinged with fear. The passengers were starting to notice, too, murmurs rippling through the cabin as the light intensified. Suddenly, the plane shook violently, sending loose objects flying.

Alarms blared in the cockpit, but no amount of training had prepared Reynolds for what came next. The glowing light expanded, enveloping the aircraft in a blinding flash.

And then, as quickly as it had come, Flight 829 vanished from the sky.

Nothing was left. No wreckage. No signal. Just silence.

CHAPTER 1

THE BERMUDA OBSESSION

Jake Carter flipped through the dusty pages of a worn-out book, his eyes scanning over faded black-and-white photographs of ships and planes that had mysteriously vanished over the Bermuda Triangle. His bedroom, cluttered with maps, books, and printouts, felt more like a conspiracy theorist's den than a typical fifteen-year-old's. But Jake wasn't typical. He had a curiosity that bordered on obsession, especially when it came to mysteries.

Outside, the Miami sun was blazing, but Jake was more interested in the swirling mass of clouds depicted on the satellite images on his computer screen. He zoomed in, eyes narrowed as he traced the outline of the Bermuda Triangle on a digital map. His fingers tapped the edge of his desk, mimicking the rhythm of the ticking wall clock. His room might have been in the middle of suburban safety, but his mind was far off, drifting somewhere over the Atlantic.

"Jake, come down for breakfast!" His mom's voice rang from downstairs, cutting through the quiet hum of his fan. "In a minute!" he called back, though he knew it was never just a minute. He reluctantly tore his gaze from the screen and sighed, slapping the book shut.

It wasn't like he hadn't read it a dozen times already. This one, Bermuda: The Devil's Triangle, was his favourite. It had details about the vanished Flight 829 from the 1970s, one of the most compelling mysteries of the Triangle—a plane that disappeared mid-flight without a trace.

He stood up and stretched, finally abandoning his lair of puzzles and theories. As he walked downstairs, his mind wandered back to Flight 829. The last recorded communication was cryptic static, followed by a loud humming sound and nothing. There was no distress call, no Mayday, just... nothing. How could a plane full of people vanish into thin air?

His mom was waiting for him at the kitchen table, already dishing scrambled eggs. She gave him a pointed look as he sat down. "You know, for someone who's so curious about mysteries, you're not very good at figuring out when your food's getting cold," she said, smirking. "Sorry, Mom," Jake mumbled, grabbing a fork. He didn't want to admit that the mystery of his life right now was finding time to balance his obsession with the Triangle and everything else. School, chores, and hanging out with friends seemed secondary to unravelling the truth.

His mom sat across from him, watching him for a moment. "You're thinking about it again, aren't you? The Bermuda Triangle thing?" Jake shrugged, not sure if he wanted to get into it. His mom was supportive, but even she had her limits. "Yeah, just some new theories I was reading up on." His mom sighed. "Jake, I know you love this stuff, but don't you think focusing on it so much is a little unhealthy? There's a whole world that isn't about mysterious disappearances."

Jake gave her a half-smile. "Yeah, but the mystery is the fun part. If we didn't have things to solve, the world would be boring, don't you think?" "Maybe, but you're not going to find all the answers online or in those old books," she said, hinting toward the pile of reading material Jake had brought downstairs days earlier and never cleaned up.

Jake opened his mouth to reply, but his phone buzzed on the table. He grabbed it and saw a message from his best friend, Maya.

Maya: Dude, you entered that contest, right? The essay one?

Weeks ago, Maya had told him about a school competition where students could write about any historical mystery, and the winner would get an all-expenses-paid trip to the Bahamas. Jake had chosen the Bermuda Triangle, of course, and had been more excited about the possibility of investigating the mystery firsthand than the actual trip itself. But the results weren't due for another week, so why was Maya messaging him now?

Jake: Yeah, why?

Maya: Dude, you won.

Jake stared at the screen, blinking in disbelief. "No way..." he muttered. His mom raised her eyebrow. "What's going on?" Jake looked up, a grin spreading across his face.

"I won. I won the contest. I'm going to the Bahamas!" His mom's eyes widened, a mix of surprise and excitement. "Really? That's fantastic, Jake! I knew you'd win. You worked so hard on that essay."

Jake's mind was already racing. The Bahamas meant flying over the Bermuda Triangle. What if— just what if—he could see something for himself, find something no one else had? This was the chance of a lifetime. His heart was racing at the thought of seeing the Devil's Triangle.

Later that day

Jake couldn't contain his excitement as he met with Maya at their usual hangout spot, a small café near the school. Maya was already there, sipping an iced coffee, her long black hair pulled into a messy bun. She laughed as Jake practically skidded to a stop in front of her. "So, Mr. Contest Winner," she said, grinning. "I guess that means you get to play detective in the Triangle, huh?"

Jake flopped into the chair across from her. "You bet! This is my shot, Maya. I get to go there. Fly over the Triangle. I mean, what are the odds? Maybe I'll see something no one else has." Maya chuckled, shaking her head. "You and your mysteries. You know, most people would be excited about the beaches, not the chance of being sucked into some supernatural vortex."

"That's what makes me different," Jake said with a playful smirk. "Besides, aren't you a little curious? I mean, think about it. All those disappearances—

ships, planes, people. There has to be something to it." Maya rolled her eyes, though she found Jake's enthusiasm amusing. "Yeah, sure. I'm curious, but I'm not the one obsessed with proving it. Besides, someone's gotta keep you grounded when you start talking about aliens and time loops."

Jake laughed. "Fair point." He hesitated for a moment before leaning in closer, lowering his voice. "But seriously, Maya, this could be big. What if I find something? Something no one else has been able to explain?" Maya leaned back in her chair, raising her hands in mock surrender. "Alright, alright, Sherlock. You've convinced me. Just don't get yourself lost in the Triangle, okay? I'd hate to have to come to rescue you."

Jake grinned. "I'll try not to. But, you know, you could always come with me. There's still an open spot." Maya's eyes widened. "Wait, what?" "Yeah. The contest allows me to bring one guest. And, who better to have by my side than my best friend?" Maya stared at him, caught off guard. "You're serious?" "Dead serious," Jake replied. "Come on, Maya. Think about it. A free trip to the Bahamas. We can solve the mystery of the Bermuda Triangle together."

Maya hesitated, clearly unsure. "I don't know,

Jake. You know I'm not as into this stuff as you are."

"I know," Jake said, "but it'll be fun. And besides, we can still hang out on the beach, go snorkelling, and all that good stuff.

It's not just about the mystery." Maya sighed, a small smile tugging at her lips. "Fine, you win. I'll go with you." Jake pumped his fist in the air triumphantly. "Yes! This is going to be epic!"

A few days later

The rest of the week flew by in a blur. Between packing, getting the necessary travel documents, and texting Maya every five minutes about what they would do once they got to the Bahamas, Jake could hardly sit still. The reality of it was finally sinking in—he was about to fly directly over the Bermuda Triangle.

On the morning of their departure, Jake stood in his room, looking at his open suitcase. He'd packed the essentials—clothes, sunscreen, his camera—but he couldn't shake the feeling that he was missing something. His eyes drifted to his desk, where his journal lay, filled with notes, sketches, and theories about the Bermuda Triangle. He grabbed it and stuffed it into his bag. He wasn't going on just any vacation. This was an investigation, and he needed to be prepared.

Downstairs, his mom was waiting by the door, holding her phone to take a picture. "Come on, smile!" she called as Jake and his suitcase trudged down the stairs. "Mom, do I have to?" Jake groaned. "Yes, really! It's not every day my son goes off on an adventure," she said, snapping a photo anyway. As Jake said his goodbyes and went to the airport, his heart raced excitedly. This was it. The trip he'd been waiting for.

Little did he know this would be the adventure of a lifetime, unravelling more than just a mystery.

CHAPTER 2

INTO THE TRIANGLE

Jake clutched his boarding pass as he stood at Gate 24 of Miami International Airport, his heart pounding with excitement and nerves. The reality of the trip was finally hitting him—he was about to fly straight into the Bermuda Triangle. He and Maya barely spoke during the car ride, but he knew they were thinking the same thing: What if something happened? What if they didn't return?

The terminal was buzzing with the usual airport chaos: travellers rushing to catch flights, families juggling suitcases, and flight attendants making their final boarding calls. But for Jake, it all faded into the background as he stared at the massive windows, watching planes take off into the bright blue sky.

"Still think we'll vanish into another dimension?"

Maya's voice asked suddenly, pulling him back to the present. He turned to see her leaning against a pillar, arms crossed, one eyebrow raised in her usual scepticism. She was trying to play it cool, but Jake could tell she was nervous, too. He smiled. "Statistically, we're more likely to get struck by lightning than disappear into the Triangle," he said, trying to sound reassuring.

Maya snorted. "Yeah, well, tell that to Flight 829." Jake glanced at her, the mention of the ill-fated flight making his stomach twist slightly. He had read everything there was to know about Flight 829, the mysterious plane that had vanished in the 1970s over the Bermuda Triangle without a trace. No debris, no distress signal—just gone.

"Well, we'll be flying right over where it disappeared," Jake said, trying to keep his voice steady. "Maybe we'll finally figure out what happened." Maya rolled her eyes, but Jake could tell she was intrigued. "You're way too excited about this," she said, shaking her head.

Before Jake could respond, the intercom crackled to life, announcing that their flight was ready for boarding. His heart raced as he grabbed his backpack, double-checking that his journal and camera were inside. He felt like a detective preparing for a big case—this was his chance to uncover something big, maybe even solve the mystery of the Bermuda Triangle.

Both excited and anxious, Jake and Maya lined up, laughing the entire way to the aircraft sky ramp. As they boarded the plane, they looked back at the terminal. Jake settled into his window seat, adjusting his backpack under the seat before him. Maya sat beside him, already pulling out her headphones and a book, clearly trying to distract herself from the nerves. Outside the window, the plane's wings gleamed in the sunlight, and beyond that, the endless expanse of blue ocean stretched toward the horizon. Somewhere out there was the Bermuda Triangle, waiting.

As the plane taxied down the runway and finally lifted off, Jake stared out the window, his heart pounding. The city of Miami quickly shrank beneath them, replaced by the sparkling Atlantic. The flight attendants made their usual announcements, but Jake barely heard them. His mind was elsewhere, racing with thoughts about the Triangle and the countless theories he had read.

"Don't look so serious," Maya said, nudging him with her elbow. "We're not even close to the Triangle yet. Relax." Jake forced a smile. "I know, I know.

I'm just... thinking." "Yeah, well, maybe think about something other than mysterious disappearances. I don't know, but are we going to the Bahamas? Beaches, sunshine, no school for a week?"

Jake chuckled, though his mind was still preoccupied. "Okay, okay. I'll try." But as the plane cruised over the ocean, Jake couldn't help but feel a strange sense of unease growing in the pit of his stomach. It wasn't fear—more like anticipation, like something was about to happen. He glanced around the cabin, noticing that everything seemed... normal. The passengers were chatting or dozing off, the flight attendants were preparing drink carts, and there was no sign of anything unusual.

Still, Jake couldn't shake the feeling that they were being watched. He returned to the window, staring at the vast ocean below. The water was calm, reflecting the sunlight like a mirror. Still, Jake knew that beneath the surface lay endless mysteries—ships lost forever, planes that vanished without a trace, stories that had haunted sailors and pilots for centuries.

"What are you thinking about now?" Maya asked, pulling one earbud out as she looked over at him. Jake was unsure of how to explain the strange feeling he had. Before Jake could respond, the intercom crackled again, and the captain's voice came over the speakers. "Ladies and gentlemen, this is your captain speaking. We've reached our cruising altitude of 35,000 feet and should fly over the Bermuda Triangle shortly. Please sit back, relax, and enjoy the flight."

Jake's heart skipped a beat. This was it. They were entering the Triangle. He pressed his face against the window, his eyes scanning the horizon for any sign of anything that might explain the strange phenomena of the Triangle. But all he saw was the same endless expanse of ocean.

Minutes ticked by, and the plane continued to cruise smoothly through the sky. Jake could feel his excitement fading, replaced by a growing disappointment. Maybe Maya was right. Maybe there was nothing here—just another ocean with an overblown reputation. Something caught his eye just as he was about to turn away from the window.

A flash of light, far below, streaked across the water's surface. "What was that?" Jake whispered, leaning closer to the glass. Maya glanced over, frowning. "What was what?" "I saw something down there," Jake said, hushed. "It looked like... I don't know, a flash or something." Maya sighed. "It's probably just the sun reflecting off the water."

But Jake wasn't convinced. He kept his eyes glued to the window, scanning the ocean for other signs. His heart raced as he thought about all the stories he had read—the strange lights, the magnetic anomalies, the compasses that spun out of control. Could this be it? Could they be seeing something connected to the Triangle?

As he stared, something else appeared on the horizon. A cloud—dark, swirling, and impossibly large. "Look," Jake said, his voice rising. "Do you see that?" Maya followed his gaze, her expression shifting from boredom to concern. "What the heck is that?"

The cloud loomed ahead of them, growing larger by the second. It was unlike any storm Jake had ever seen—it seemed almost alive, twisting and writhing as it moved across the sky. Lightning crackled within its depths, illuminating the dark mass with brief flashes of eerie light.

The plane began to shake, turbulence jolting them in their seats. The flight attendants hurried down the aisle, instructing passengers to fasten their seatbelts. Jake's excitement quickly turned to fear as the plane continued to tremble. "This isn't normal," Jake muttered, gripping the armrests of his seat. Maya looked pale, her hands clutching the edge of her seat. "You think?"

The captain's voice came over the intercom again, but this time, it was different—strained, tense. "Ladies and gentlemen, we're experiencing some unexpected turbulence. Please remain seated with your seatbelts fastened. We're doing everything to escape this as quickly as possible."

Jake's heart pounded in his chest. He glanced at Maya, who was staring wide-eyed at the window. The dark cloud was closing in on them, engulfing the plane in swirling shadows. The turbulence worsened, shaking the plane violently. Passengers around them were murmuring in fear, some gripping their armrests, others holding hands with their loved ones.

Suddenly, the plane lurched to the side, sending a tray of drinks crashing to the floor. Jake's stomach flipped as the cabin lights flickered, plunging them into semi-darkness. The air was tense, the engines roaring as the plane struggled against the storm. "This is bad," Jake whispered, his knuckles turning white as he clutched his seat.

Maya didn't respond, her eyes wide with terror. The plane shook harder this time as if an invisible force tossed it around. The storm outside the window was unlike anything Jake had ever seen;

lightning flashed in strange, unnatural patterns, casting eerie shadows across the cabin.

Jake's mind raced, trying to make sense of what was happening. Could this be the Bermuda Triangle? Was this one of the unexplained phenomena he had read about? Magnetic anomalies, rogue waves, strange weather patterns—it all seemed like science fiction. Still, in the middle of it, it felt terrifyingly real.

As the plane shuddered again, the captain's voice came over the intercom, but this time, it was barely audible, drowned out by static and the storm's roar. "...attempting to... out of... hold on..." Jake strained to hear, but the words were lost as the static drowned out his words. The plane continued to rattle, its engines groaning as it powered through the storm, trying to escape its grip.

Just as Jake thought things couldn't get worse, the cabin was filled with a blinding flash of light. For a moment, everything was illuminated in stark white, and then—total darkness. The plane fell silent, except for the panicked gasps of passengers. The lights flickered back on, casting a dim glow over the cabin. Jake's heart raced as he turned to Maya, who was gripping her seat with trembling hands.

"What just happened?" she whispered, her voice difficult to hear over the engines. Jake shook his head, unable to find the words to answer. His mind was reeling, trying to process what they had just witnessed. Was it lightning? A freak electrical surge? Or something else entirely? Before he could say anything, the plane gave another violent lurch, sending his stomach flipping again. He felt the sensation of weightlessness as the plane dipped suddenly, as if they were plummeting toward the ocean below.

Then, just as quickly as it had begun, the turbulence stopped. The plane levelled out, the shaking ceased, and the storm outside the windows seemed to vanish. It was as if they had passed through some invisible barrier, leaving the chaos behind. Jake blinked in disbelief. The dark cloud looming ahead was gone, replaced by a clear, calm sky. The ocean below was still and serene, as if nothing had happened.

"What... what was that?" Maya asked, her voice shaking. Jake shook his head, still trying to make sense of it. "I don't know. That was..." "Insane," Maya finished for him, her eyes wide. "That was insane." Jake nodded but couldn't shake the feeling that something had changed. The air in the cabin felt different, heavier somehow. He glanced at the other passengers, who were murmuring to each other in hushed, nervous voices. The flight attendants were moving quickly through the aisle, checking on everyone, but their expressions were tight, their smiles forced.

Jake's hand instinctively went to his backpack, feeling for the camera he had packed. He had to document this—whatever "this" was. Something had happened, something beyond explanation. And Jake knew, deep down, that they weren't out of the woods yet.

Jake's mind raced with possibilities as the plane continued to cruise through the now-clear skies. Had they just experienced one of the infamous Bermuda Triangle phenomena? Magnetic interference, time distortion, some atmospheric anomaly? It all seemed too surreal, but the evidence was right there—he had seen it with his own eyes.

"We need to be ready," Jake said quietly, his gaze still fixed out the window. Maya frowned. "Ready for what?" Jake turned to her; his expression serious. "For whatever happens next."

The rest of the flight passed uneventfully, much to Jake and Maya's surprise. They landed in Nassau without further incident, and the passengers disembarked, looking dazed and confused. Jake could feel the suspense as people whispered to each other, clearly shaken by the turbulence and the strange storm they had passed through.

Jake's phone buzzed with a notification when they stepped off the plane. He pulled it out, expecting a message from his parents or a news alert about the storm, but instead, he was greeted with something far stranger. The date on his phone read March 24th. Jake frowned, glancing at Maya. "That can't be right," he muttered. "It's supposed to be March 22nd."

Maya pulled out her phone, her expression mirroring his confusion. "What the...?" Jake's heart began to race again. How could two days have passed? The flight had only been a few hours, and they hadn't crossed any significant time zones. Yet somehow, they had lost two entire days. "This is impossible," Jake whispered, his mind racing with possibilities. Had they been unconscious? Was this some glitch? Or was it something more sinister connected to the Bermuda Triangle?

Maya's voice was shaky as she checked her messages. "My mom's been texting me, asking where we've been. She thought we were missing." Jake's stomach turned. Missing. That word hung in the air like a dark cloud, echoing all the stories he had read about planes and ships vanishing in the

Triangle.

"We need to find out what happened," Jake said, his voice low but urgent. "We need to know what's going on." Maya nodded, still looking shaken. "Yeah... but how?" Jake wasn't sure, but one thing was clear: they wouldn't find answers standing around in an airport. He felt that whatever had happened to them on that flight was just the beginning.

The ride to their hotel was quiet. Both were lost in their thoughts. Jake kept glancing out the window, scanning the horizon for any sign of the strange storm they had passed through, but the sky was clear. It was as if the storm—and the two days they had lost—had never happened.

When they arrived at the hotel, the sun began to set, casting a warm golden glow over the island. But even the beauty of the Bahamas couldn't shake Jake's unease. He knew he couldn't relax until he figured out what had happened. As they checked into their room, Jake pulled out his camera and journal, determined to document every flight detail.

He flipped through the photos he had taken, hoping to find anything that could explain what they had experienced. But the photos showed nothing unusual: just clouds, the ocean, and the inside of the plane. Maya sat on the bed, scrolling through her phone. "There's nothing online about any storms," she said, her voice tight. "No news, no weather alerts, nothing." "That's impossible. We flew right through it. It should be all over the news."

Maya shrugged, looking just as confused as he felt. "Maybe... maybe it wasn't a regular storm." Jake set the camera down, his mind racing. If it hadn't been a regular storm, then what was it? A magnetic anomaly? Some time distortion? He had read theories about the Bermuda Triangle causing disruptions in the space-time continuum, but those were just theories—wild, unproven ideas.

Yet here they were. Two days gone, with no explanation. "We need to talk to the other passengers," Jake said, standing up. "See if anyone else noticed anything." Maya agreed, but Jake could tell she was still processing everything. "Yeah, good idea. But what if no one else remembers?"

Jake paused, considering her words. What if they were the only ones who had noticed? What if, for everyone else, it had been a perfectly normal flight? The thought sent a chill down his spine. "We'll find out," he said, grabbing his journal and heading for the door. "One way or another, we'll figure this out."

As they left the room and headed back to the

lobby, Jake couldn't shake the feeling that they were on the verge of discovering something incredible that could change everything they thought they knew about the world.

CHAPTER 3

THE ISLAND'S SECRETS

Jake and Maya descended the narrow hotel corridor, heading toward the lobby. The once-exciting idea of being in the Bahamas had soured, replaced by an unsettling dread. The other guests were still back in their rooms, and Jake couldn't help but wonder if they had noticed something strange. The flight—the storm—the missing time. Nothing made sense, and he was determined to find out why.

As they stepped into the lobby, the eerie silence hit them again. The lobby was empty—no staff, no other guests, no sounds except the faint hum of the ceiling fans. It was as if the resort had been abandoned. "Where is everyone?" Maya whispered, her voice echoing slightly in the large, open space.

Jake shook his head, glancing around nervously.

The reception desk was unstaffed, the doors to the dining area were shut tightly, and the only light came from the dim bulbs hanging overhead. "This place is starting to creep me out," Maya added, folding her arms over her chest. "Yeah," Jake agreed. "Something's definitely off, where is everyone?"

They approached the reception desk, Jake reaching out hesitantly to ring the bell on the counter. The sound echoed through the empty lobby, but no one responded. Jake rang it again, louder this time. Still, nothing.

Maya was pacing, watching nervously at the doors leading outside. "Maybe we should just leave," she suggested. "Find a different hotel, or... I don't know, go back to the airport?"

Jake considered it for a moment. The idea of leaving this strange place was tempting, but something held him back. He had come here to solve a mystery, and now that mystery had become very real. Whatever was happening here—whatever had caused the storm and the lost time—was something he needed to understand.

"We can't leave," Jake said, more to himself than to Maya. "Not yet. We need to figure out what's going on." Maya stopped pacing and looked at him, worry etched across her face. "Jake, what if we're in over our heads? I mean, this isn't some school project. This is real now."

Jake replied, "I know. But we've already seen too much. If we leave now, we might never get the chance to understand what happened. And what if it happens to someone else?" Maya nodded reluctantly. "Okay. But where do we even start?" Jake looked around the lobby again, searching for clues that might give them a lead.

That's when he noticed something strange—a small, old-fashioned key sitting on the counter, partially hidden under a stack of papers. He picked it up, turning it over in his hand.

The key was tarnished, and its brass surface had worn smoothly from years of use. "What do you think it opens?" Maya asked, peering over his shoulder. "No idea," Jake replied, frowning. "But it looks like it's been here a long time."

Before he could say anything else, the glass doors leading to the outside suddenly blew open, a gust of warm, salty air rushing into the lobby. Jake and Maya jumped, startled by the sudden noise. The doors banged against the walls, then slowly swung back and forth on their hinges. "Did you feel that?" Maya asked, her voice trembling.

"Yeah, that was very weird. I wonder what caused that", he replied. The wind had been strong, almost unnatural, as if it had been pushing them—urging them to leave the hotel and venture outside. He glanced at Maya, who looked just as uneasy as he felt. "Maybe we should follow it," Jake suggested, unsure what to say.

Maya agreed. "Okay. But let's stick together, no splitting up and you have a deal." They walked toward the open doors, the wind whipping through their hair as they stepped outside. The resort grounds were spookily quiet, the palm trees swaying gently in the breeze. The sun was high in the sky, but the air felt thick, like a storm looming just beyond the horizon.

Jake glanced around the area for anything unusual. The resort was on a small island, isolated from the mainland by miles of open ocean. The beach was just a short walk away, and beyond that, the dense jungle that covered most of the island. "Which way?" Maya asked, her voice tinged with fear.

Jake looked toward the jungle, feeling a strange pull in that direction. "The jungle," he said decisively. "There's something in there—something we need to find." "Lead the way", Maya replied. They made their way down the path that led from the resort to the edge of the jungle.

The sandy path they were walking on quickly turned into a jungle full of thick plants and tall palm trees. These trees and vines stretched up high, forming a leafy roof blocking most of the sunlight. The air became sticky and humid, making it harder to breathe. All around them, the sounds of the island felt closer and louder. They could hear the distant roar of the ocean waves, the gentle rustling of leaves as the wind moved through the trees, and sometimes the sharp call of a bird echoing through the jungle.

As they ventured deeper into the jungle, the path became less defined, the vegetation growing thicker and more tangled. Jake pushed aside a large frond, revealing a small clearing up ahead.

The ground was littered with debris—old crates, rusted metal, and what looked like wooden boat pieces. Jake's heart skipped a beat. This wasn't just any clearing—it was a graveyard of forgotten things, remnants of past visitors stranded on the island, just like them.

"This place is a wreck," Maya said in a low voice. "What do you think happened here?" Jake knelt, examining one of the wooden crates. It was partially buried in the sand, its sides splintered and worn by time. He could make out faded letters stencilled on the side: "SS Vanguard." He stood up, looking around at the many other pieces of debris that lay in the clearing. "USS Cyclops, SS El Faro, TK183, they're all here!" Jake said loudly in an excited tone. "What exactly are they?" Maya asked. "Lost ships and planes in the Devil's Triangle that have been recorded in history."

Maya's eyes widened. "You mean... they never made it back?" Jake nodded slowly. "Yeah. And we might not either." Maya shuddered, wrapping her arms around herself. "Jake, we need to get out of here. This place isn't safe." Jake stood up, brushing the sand from his hands and knees. "Not yet. There's something we need to find first."

Maya stared at him, fear and uncertainty in her eyes. "What if we can't get back?" Jake looked at her, unsure how to respond. "We will. But we need to figure out what's happening on this island first. If we don't, we'll never know the truth." Maya sighed but nodded reluctantly. "Okay. But let's be quick."

They kept moving through the thick jungle, following a path that twisted and wound deeper into the island. The further they went, the more the trees and plants seemed to close in around them, making the trail narrower and more challenging to navigate. Jake's sense of unease grew with every step as if the jungle itself was alive and watching them from the shadows. He couldn't shake the feeling that the eyes were on them, hidden in the dense greenery. He glanced over at Maya, who was nervously looking around at the towering trees and tangled vines, her eyes wide with worry.

Every rustle of leaves or twig snap seemed to make her jump, as though she was expecting something to leap out at them at any moment. They walked silently, the sounds of the jungle growing louder, making them feel even more isolated and alone as they ventured deeper into the island's mysterious heart.

The jungle seemed to close in around them, the trees growing taller and more twisted, their branches intertwining overhead to form a natural tunnel. The light grew dimmer, the air cooler as if they were descending into some forgotten world. Suddenly, the path opened into a large clearing. Jake stopped in his tracks, his breath catching in his throat.

The clearing was dominated by a massive stone structure, half-buried in the earth and overgrown with vines and moss. It looked ancient, like something out of a lost civilization.

"What is this place?" Maya whispered; her eyes wide with wonder. Jake shook his head, unable to tear his eyes away from the structure. "I don't know. But it looks important." They approached the stone structure cautiously, their footsteps echoing in the silence.

The stone was weathered and cracked, covered in strange symbols and carvings that seemed to pulse with an otherworldly energy. Jake reached out, tracing his fingers over one of the symbols. It felt warm to the touch, almost alive.

"Jake, look," Maya said, pointing to the structure's base. Jake followed her gaze with his eyes. There, partially buried in the earth, was a metal object—rusted and worn but unmistakable. It was the wing of a plane, the letters "N829" barely visible on its surface. "This... this is from Flight 829," Jake whispered, his voice trembling. "It's here."

Maya stared at the wreckage, her face pale. "But how? How could it be here?" Jake shook his head, his mind racing. "I don't know. But this proves it— this island is where everything that disappears in the Bermuda Triangle ends up. Ships, planes, people... they're all brought here." Maya looked around, "Jake, we need to leave. Now."

But Jake couldn't move. He was transfixed by the symbols on the stone structure, his mind drawn to the mystery of what lay beneath the surface. There was something here—something powerful and ancient—and it was calling him. "We can't leave yet," Jake said, his voice distant.

Maya grabbed his arm, shaking him. "Jake, snap out of it! We need to go!" He looked at Maya, her eyes wide with fear, and realized she was right. They needed to leave—before it was too late.

"Okay," Jake said, his voice steadying. "You're right. Let's get out of here." But as they turned to leave, the air around them grew thick, almost suffocating. The shadows cast by the twisted trees seemed to deepen, and a low hum began to resonate from the stone structure behind them.

Jake froze, feeling the hairs on his neck stand up. Maya gripped his arm tighter, her nails digging into his skin. "What's happening?" she whispered, her voice trembling.

Jake didn't answer. He was too focused on the strange vibrations coursing through the ground beneath their feet as if the island was coming to life. The hum grew louder, filling the air with energy. It was as if the fabric of reality was being warped, twisted by some unseen force. And then, out of his eye, Jake saw movement.

A shadow, darker than the rest, slipping through the trees at the edge of the clearing. He turned his head sharply, but it was gone. His heart raced, the sense of being watched more intense than ever. "We need to move," Jake said urgently, pulling Maya. But before they could step, the ground beneath them began to tremble.

The stone structure groaned, the ancient carvings glowing faintly as the vibrations intensified. The metal wreckage at its base rattled and shifted as if pulled by an invisible force. Jake's pulse quickened. This wasn't just some abandoned ruin—there was something alive here, something powerful and ancient that they had disturbed.

"Run!" Jake shouted, his voice breaking through the noise. He and Maya bolted toward the path they had come from, the ground shaking violently beneath them. The jungle seemed to close around them, the trees swaying and groaning as if protesting their escape.

The hum grew louder as they ran, resonating deep within Jake's chest. He didn't dare look back, but he could feel it—a presence, dark and malevolent, following them, hunting them. The path twisted and turned, branches whipping at their faces as they sprinted through the dense foliage.

Finally, they burst out of the jungle and into the clearing near the beach, gasping for breath. The trembling stopped, the hum faded, and the air seemed to lighten as if whatever had been chasing them had retreated into the jungle. Jake doubled over, hands on his knees as he tried to catch his breath. His heart was pounding so hard he thought it might burst out of his chest. Maya was beside him, breathing heavily, her face pale with fear.

"What... what was that?" she gasped. Jake shook his head, unable to form the words. He had never felt anything like it—the sheer power and terror gripping him. It was as if the island was responding to their presence in a way that defied explanation. "I don't know," Jake finally managed to say, his voice shaky. "But we need to get off this island. Now."

"Agreed. But how? There's no one here—no staff, no boats, nothing." Jake straightened up, glancing around the deserted resort. The pristine beach and crystal-clear waters now seemed like a cruel joke, hiding a darkness beneath the surface. They were trapped on an island that shouldn't exist, where time seemed to bend and break.

"We'll find a way," Jake said, more to reassure

himself than anything. "We have to." They returned to the resort, their senses on high alert for any sign of danger. The lobby was still empty, the silence unnerving. Jake and Maya headed straight for the small office behind the reception desk, hoping to find anything to help them understand what was happening.

The office was cluttered with papers, maps, and old documents, most yellowed with age. A large map of the island was pinned to the wall, marked with various symbols and notes. Jake scanned it, his eyes landing on a particular area near the island's centre, where a red X had been drawn.

"What's this?" Jake muttered, tracing the map with his finger. Maya peered over in his direction. "Looks like some landmark. Maybe it's important?" Jake nodded, his mind racing. The X was near where they had found the stone structure.

Could it be connected to the strange energy they had felt? Was something buried there that could explain the island's mysteries? "We need to check it out," Jake said decisively. "It might be our only way out."

Maya looked at him, her expression torn. "Are you sure? After what just happened..." "This island is dangerous, Maya. We need to understand what's happening here to get out alive." Maya sighed but looked to agree. "Okay. But let's be careful." They left the office and headed back toward the jungle with the map clutched tightly in Jake's hand. The path they had taken earlier was still there, but the once beautiful scenery now seemed ominous, hiding secrets that could easily consume them. "I wonder where all the people are. I haven't seen a single person since we left the resort," Jake said aloud.

CHAPTER 4

STRANGE ENCOUNTERS

As they approached the clearing with the stone structure again, Jake felt the air grow heavier once more, the same energy they had felt earlier returning. But this time, he was ready. They had to face whatever was on this island head-on. The stone structure loomed ahead of them, its ancient carvings pulsing faintly with a strange light. The wreckage from Flight 829 was still there, half-buried in the earth, as if it had been there for centuries.

Jake took a deep breath and stepped forward, clutching the hotel key in his hand. He didn't know what it would unlock, but he felt sure it was connected to whatever force controlled the island. As he approached the structure, the ground began to tremble again, and the hum returned, louder and more insistent.

But this time, Jake didn't back down. He pressed forward, the key growing warm in his hand as if reacting to the energy around it. The carvings on the stone seemed to shift and change before his eyes, forming symbols and patterns that were both alien and familiar.

Maya grabbed his arm. "Jake, what are you doing?" Jake didn't answer. He was transfixed by the glowing symbols, drawn toward them by an invisible force. He reached out with the key, pressing it into a small indentation in the stone.

For a moment, nothing happened. Then, with a loud rumble, the ground beneath them split open, revealing a hidden chamber below. The stone structure shifted, sliding back to reveal a dark staircase descending into the earth. Maya gasped, stepping back in shock. "Jake, what did you do?" Jake stared down into the darkness, his heart racing. "I think... I found the way in."

Maya looked at him, fear in her eyes. "Are you seriously thinking of going down there?" Jake turned to her, his face full of curiosity. "If we want to get out of here, we need to know what we're dealing with. This is our only chance." Maya nodded reluctantly. "Okay. But if anything happens..."

Jake placed a hand on her shoulder, trying to

reassure her. "We'll be fine. We must be." With that, they descended into the darkness, the stone staircase creaking beneath their feet. The air grew colder, and the chamber walls dampened and slicked with moisture. The hum grew louder, filling their ears and vibrating through their bones.

As they reached the bottom, they found themselves in a large, circular chamber, the walls covered in the same strange symbols they had seen on the stone structure above.

In the centre of the chamber stood a large stone pedestal on which a glowing crystal pulsed with an eerie light. Jake approached it cautiously, his eyes wide with awe and fear. This was it—the source of the island's power. The crystal seemed to radiate an almost hypnotic energy, drawing him closer.

But a cold and menacing voice echoed through the chamber before he could touch it. "Who dares disturb the Keeper?" Jake froze, his blood running cold. He turned slowly, his eyes searching the shadows for the source of the voice. Maya clung to his arm, her face pale with terror. Out of the darkness, a figure emerged, tall and cloaked in black, its face hidden beneath a hood. The air around them seemed to freeze, the energy becoming almost unbearable.

"You have trespassed where you do not belong," the figure hissed, its voice echoing through the chamber. "This island is a place of secrets, and those who seek them out do not leave." Jake swallowed hard, his mind racing. This was the Keeper—the being controlling the island that had brought them here. He had read about it in the journals, the legends of an ancient guardian that protected the Bermuda Triangle's secrets.

"We didn't mean to disturb anything," Jake said, his voice trembling. "We just want to understand... and get home." The Keeper laughed, a sound that sent chills down Jake's spine. "Home? You are far from home, boy. The only way off this island is through the truth. But beware—some truths are better left buried." Jake exchanged a nervous glance with Maya, then returned to the Keeper. "What do we have to do?"

The Keeper pointed to the crystal. "Unlock the secrets of the island. But know this—once you start, there is no turning back." Jake was scared. The crystal pulsed with an eerie light, casting shadows that danced across the chamber's walls. Maya gripped his arm tightly, her breath shallow and rapid. The Keeper's presence filled the room, an ominous force that seemed to drain the very warmth from the air.

"What does it mean to unlock the secrets of the island?" Jake asked, his voice barely above a whisper. The Keeper's hooded figure did not move, but its voice echoed through the chamber, as cold as the grave. "To unlock the secrets is to face the truths buried deep within this place. Truths have claimed the lives and souls of those who came before you. The island does not give up its secrets easily."

Jake's heart pounded in his chest. He had come here seeking answers, but now he was faced with a choice that could determine whether they would ever leave this island. He glanced at Maya, whose fear mirrored his own, and then back at the crystal. "What if we don't do it?" Maya asked, her voice trembling. The Keeper's laugh was low and menacing. "If you do not, you will remain here, as all the others before you have. This island is a place where time bends and reality warps. It is not a place where you can walk away."

He had to know the truth, even if it meant facing whatever horrors lay ahead. He took a deep breath and stepped closer to the pedestal, reaching for the crystal. The light grew brighter, the hum louder, as if the island was reacting to his decision. As his fingers closed around the crystal, a surge of energy shot through him, filling him with a strange sensation—part fear, part exhilaration. The chamber around them seemed to dissolve, replaced by visions—flashes of the past, the island's history, and those trapped here before them.

Jake saw glimpses of ships torn apart by storms, planes spiralling out of control, and people wandering the jungle in despair, lost in time. He saw the stone structure being built by hands long forgotten, the crystal placed at its centre as a beacon—a key to another realm. And he saw the Keeper, watching the island, ensuring its secrets remained hidden.

The visions came faster and faster, overwhelming Jake's senses. He felt as though he was being pulled into the very heart of the island, into the depths of its darkest secrets. The ground beneath him seemed to give way, and he was falling, spiralling into the unknown.

But then, just as suddenly as it began, it stopped. Jake gasped, releasing the crystal and stumbling back. The chamber was silent again, and the visions were gone, leaving only the cold, glum reality of the island. The Keeper's voice broke the silence, its tone now tinged with something that almost resembled satisfaction. "You have begun the journey. The truth is within your grasp, but beware—this is only the beginning. The island will test, challenge, and show you the darkest parts of yourself. If you survive, you may find the way home. If not..."

Jake turned to Maya, who was staring at him with wide eyes. "Jake, what did you see?" Jake shook his head, still reeling from the experience. "Everything. The island, the disappearances, the people who were trapped here. This place... it's like a crossroads where different times and realities intersect. The Keeper, it's been here for centuries, guarding the island's secrets."

Maya shivered, rubbing the sides of her arms. "But why? Why does it keep people here?" Jake glanced at the Keeper, who remained silent, watching them with those unseen eyes. "I don't know. But I think... I think it's all connected to that crystal. It's like a key, or maybe a beacon, that ties this place to the Bermuda Triangle. If we can figure out how to use it, maybe we can find a way out."

Maya's expression remained doubtful. "And what about the others? The people who disappeared?" "They're here, somewhere. Lost in time, maybe in a different reality. We must find them, too. We can't just leave them here." The Keeper's voice cut through their conversation. "Your time is running short. The island does not tolerate hesitation. Move forward or be consumed."

Jake turned back to the staircase, the path ahead shrouded in darkness, but with a newfound resolve. "Let's go," he said, his voice steady. Maya nodded, her fear giving way to a reluctant acceptance. Together, they ascended the stairs, leaving the chamber and the Keeper behind. The air grew warmer as they climbed, and the sounds of the jungle returned, the hum of insects and the rustle of leaves filling the night.

The jungle seemed darker now, the trees casting long shadows that flickered and danced in the moonlight. Jake glanced at Maya, who was silent, her face tense. The Keeper's warning echoed in his mind, a constant reminder of their danger. "Stay close," Jake said, leading the way back toward the resort. The path seemed different now, as if the island was shifting around them, reshaping the landscape to confuse and disorient them. They reached the edge of the jungle, the resort coming into view again. The buildings were dark, the windows empty and lifeless.

"We need to find a way to stop this," Maya whispered, her voice trembling. "Whatever it is, it's not just going to let us leave." Jake nodded, his mind racing. "There must be something we can do. The crystal, the structure—maybe there's a way to break the connection, to sever the island from the Bermuda Triangle."

They made their way back to the lobby, the spooky silence even more pronounced now that they knew what lurked in the shadows. Jake's thoughts were a whirlwind of ideas, each more desperate than the last, as he tried to devise a plan. As they entered the lobby, Jake noticed something they hadn't seen before—a map on the wall, partially hidden behind a curtain. He pulled it aside, revealing an old, faded island map. It differed from the one they had found in the office, more detailed, with markings and symbols that seemed to correspond with the stone structure they had discovered.

"This might be what we need. This could be the answer," Jake said, studying the map intently. Maya leaned in, her eyes scanning the symbols. "It looks like the map points to specific places on the island. Maybe these are the locations of the other pieces of the puzzle. If we can find them, we might be able to figure out how to break the connection."

Maya nodded, her eyes lighting up with a spark of hope. "Okay, let's do it. Grab the map, and we'll head to the first point," she said with a newfound confidence in her voice. Jake felt a rush of determination wash over him, stronger than before. The island had challenged them at every turn, throwing obstacles and dangers in their way, but they weren't about to back down. No matter how strange or dangerous things had gotten, they weren't giving up now.

Together, they were a team and would solve the mystery of the Bermuda Triangle, no matter what it took. The island had its secrets, but they were determined to uncover every one of them and find a way to escape from this cursed place. With the map in hand and a new sense of purpose, they set off, ready to face whatever lay ahead, knowing they could overcome anything if they stuck together.

As they set off into the night, the map clutched tightly in Jake's hand he knew the journey ahead would be dangerous. The island would test, challenge, and force them to confront their deepest fears. And with that thought, Jake and Maya disappeared into the darkness, the island's secrets waiting to be revealed.

CHAPTER 5

THE KEEPER'S WARNING

Jake and Maya stood at the entrance to the dark chamber. The Keeper had vanished as mysteriously as he had appeared. Jake's mind was racing as he tried to piece together what they were facing. They were trapped in a time loop, and the only way to escape was to solve the island's ancient puzzle. But how? And what did the Keeper mean by "dangerous challenges"?

"We can't just stand here," Maya said, interrupting Jake's thoughts. Her voice trembled slightly, but she was holding it together. Jake stepped into the chamber. The walls were lined with ancient carvings, like the ones they had seen on the stone structure earlier.

But these were different—more intricate, more detailed. He traced his fingers along the symbols, feeling the grooves etched into the stone.

"What do you think these mean?" Maya asked. "I'm not sure," Jake replied, squinting at the symbols. "But they must be part of the puzzle. Maybe they're instructions... or warnings." Maya shivered. "Warnings, great." The Keeper had mentioned traps and illusions—what if these symbols were the key to avoiding them? He scanned the walls, trying to make sense of the patterns. The symbols seemed to form a sequence, but it was like nothing he had ever seen before.

As he pondered the symbols, a low rumbling echoed through the chamber, the ground beneath their feet trembling. Maya grabbed Jake's shirt, her eyes wide with fear. "Did you feel that?" she whispered. Yeah, we need to move. I think the island's starting its first challenge."

Jake knew they couldn't afford to waste time. They moved deeper into the chamber, arriving at a large circular room with a massive stone disc embedded in the floor. The disc was inscribed with the same strange symbols arranged in concentric circles.

"This must be the first puzzle," Jake said, gazing at the disc. The symbols looked like they could be rotated, each clicking into place as part of a more significant mechanism.

Maya studied the disc, her face with a look of frustration. "How do we know which symbols to use? There are so many." Jake recalled the carvings on the walls, quickly looking around the dark chamber for a clue. His eyes fell on a specific set of symbols etched into the wall, arranged in a circular pattern identical to the ones on the disc. "There!" he said, pointing. "That's the combination."

They worked together, turning the symbols on the disc to match the sequence on the wall. The disc emitted a low hum with each turn as if acknowledging their progress. But just as Jake aligned the final symbol, the chamber shook violently, and the disc began to sink into the floor, revealing a dark, water-filled shaft beneath it.

"This must be related to the ships that have sunk in the triangle over the years," Maya said smartly. Jake looked impressed. Maya gasped, stepping back as the shaft continued to fill with water. The low rumble of flowing water echoed through the chamber, growing louder by the second. They had triggered something, but what? The water continued to rise, now lapping at the edges of the stone disc. "It's flooding," Jake realized. "We need to get out of here—now!"

They turned and ran without another word, retracing their steps through the chamber. But the ground was unstable, the water seeping through cracks in the walls and floor, making the path treacherous. The rising water wasn't just a threat of drowning; it was also pushing them toward the edge of panic. The water was surprisingly icy cold also.

They reached a narrow tunnel that descended deeper into the island's core. Without hesitation, they plunged into the darkness, the sound of rushing water close behind them.

The tunnel led to another chamber, but this one was different—colder, with water pooling on the floor and more seeping through the walls. "We need to find a way to stop the water," Maya said, panic edging into her voice.

Jake looked around the room desperately. In the centre of the chamber stood a large, rusted metal box on a pedestal, covered in more strange symbols. The box was old, its surface worn and corroded by time, but it was important. "This has to be part of the puzzle," Jake said, approaching the box. The symbols on its surface seemed to form a sequence, but the mechanism to open it was far from straightforward.

Jake studied the box, turning it in his hands. The

symbols moved slightly, clicking into place like a complex lock. "It's like a puzzle box," he muttered, "but we have to figure out the right combination." The water continued to rise, now covering their ankles and creeping higher. The urgency of their situation pressed on them, and Jake's hands trembled as he manipulated the symbols on the box. Each click brought a new wave of anxiety. The island was not just testing their wits but their will to survive.

Suddenly, the box emitted a soft glow, the symbols aligning in a way that suggested they were on the right track. But before they could feel relief, the walls began to crack under the pressure of the water, sending jets of water spraying into the room. The cracks grew wider, and the chamber shook violently. "Jake, hurry!" Maya shouted, her voice strained as she tried to keep her balance on the slippery floor.

Jake's focus sharpened as he made the final adjustments to the box. With a loud click, the lid sprang open, revealing a glowing crystal inside. The water around them bubbled and churned as if reacting to the crystal's energy.

Jake grabbed the crystal, feeling its warmth spread through his hand. "This must be the key. We need to use it to stop the flooding, I think."

But before they could move, the chamber trembled again, and the water surged upward, sweeping them off their feet. The current was strong, pulling them toward the centre of the room where the stone disc had been. Jake clung to the crystal with one hand, using the other to grab Maya's arm. "We have to reach the surface!" Jake shouted over the roar of the water.

They fought against the current, kicking and pushing toward the tunnel that led back to the surface. The water was rising fast, now up to their chests, and the chamber was filling rapidly. If they didn't get out soon, they would be trapped.

Maya gasped as the water surged over her head, but Jake pulled her up, his grip on the crystal tightening. The light from the crystal seemed to pulse in response, and for a moment, the water around them stilled.

"Keep going!" Jake urged, and they swam with all their strength, finally reaching the tunnel entrance. The water rushed through the tunnel, creating a powerful current that threatened to drag them back into the chamber. But they pushed on, driven by sheer willpower and the knowledge that this was their only chance.

The tunnel opened into a larger passage, and Jake could see the light ahead—daylight, streaming through an opening in the rock. With a final burst of energy, they swam toward it, the crystal still glowing in Jake's hand.

The current was relentless, but they were close—so close. With one last push, they broke through the surface, gasping for air as they emerged into a shallow pool at the base of a cliff. The water here was calm, fed by a small waterfall that trickled down from above. They pulled themselves onto the rocky shore, coughing and shivering from the cold.

Jake lay on the rocks, catching his breath, the crystal still clutched in his hand. He looked over at Maya, who was lying beside him, breathing heavily but alive. "We made it," Jake said, his voice hoarse. Maya nodded, too exhausted to speak. She stared at the sky, the reality of their ordeal sinking in. They had survived the first challenge, but the island's trials were far from over. "Are you okay?" Jake asked Maya. "Yeah, barely; we nearly drowned in there, Jake!"

"What do we do now? Is it time to sleep yet?" Maya asked through tired eyes. Jake looked at the jungle, the trees swaying gently in the breeze. The island was quiet as if waiting for them to make their next move. "We keep going," Jake said. "We find the next piece of the puzzle and figure out how to use these crystals to escape."

Maya pushed herself to her feet. "I wonder how many more challenges there are." Jake didn't have an answer. He knew only that they had to keep moving, keep solving the island's puzzles, no matter the cost. The Keeper's words echoed in his mind—this was only the beginning. As they returned to the jungle, the crystal lighting their path, Jake felt fear and drive to keep going. The island had tested them and would test them again, but they had survived. They were closer to uncovering the truth and finding a way off the island.

As they took their first steps back into the jungle, a sudden chill ran through the air, causing Jake and Maya to stop. The crystal in Jake's hand flickered, its light dimming for a moment before glowing brighter than before. The temperature dropped rapidly, and the once-gentle breeze turned into a cold gust that whipped through the trees. Out of the shadows, the Keeper materialized, his form emerging from thin air as if he had always been there, waiting. His figure was shrouded in darkness, the only visible feature being his eyes—two glowing orbs that seemed to pierce through the souls of those who gazed upon them.

"You have done well to survive the first trial," the Keeper's voice echoed, low and haunting. "But know this: the island's true test is far from over." Jake tightened his grip on the crystal, feeling its warmth, contrasting with the cold surrounding them. "What do you want from us?" Jake demanded, trying to keep his voice steady.

The Keeper's eyes flickered with something akin to amusement. "What I want is irrelevant. It is what the island requires. To escape, you must climb higher, face the wind, and walk on ropes where the ground has no hold. Only then will you find the next piece of your puzzle." Maya glanced at Jake, "What do you mean? Where are we supposed to go?"

The Keeper raised a hand, pointing to the west, where the jungle grew denser and the trees taller. "The path will reveal itself, as it always does. But beware, for the higher you climb, the further you must fall."

The image of a high, rickety rope bridge formed in his mind—a test of their balance, courage, and will to survive. The Keeper lowered his hand and stepped back, his form beginning to fade.

"One more thing," the Keeper said. "The bridge you seek is not just a path—it is a riddle in itself.

Solve it or fall into the abyss." With that, the Keeper vanished, leaving Jake and Maya alone in the cold, dark jungle. The air gradually warmed, but the lingering chill in Jake's bones remained.

Jake turned to Maya, who was visibly shaken. "We have to be ready," he said softly. "Whatever this next challenge is, we'll face it together." Maya nodded, though her eyes were still wide with fear. "I just wish I knew how many more of these challenges there were." Jake looked westward, the direction the Keeper had indicated. "We'll find out soon enough. Come on, let's go."

As they made their way deeper into the jungle, following the path the Keeper had hinted at, Jake felt they were getting closer to the answer and finding their way back home.

CHAPTER 6

CLIMBING HIGHER

The jungle thickened as Jake and Maya pressed forward, their nerves still raw from the Keeper's ominous warning. The air grew cooler with each step, and the underbrush seemed to whisper with secrets of its own. Overhead, the canopy began to thin, revealing glimpses of a rapidly dark sky, though it wasn't yet late in the day.

Jake felt the crystal in his pocket; its pulse synchronized with his heartbeat. The Keeper's cryptic instructions played repeatedly in his mind—"climb higher, face the wind, and walk on ropes where the ground has no hold." He knew that whatever awaited them next would be more dangerous than they had already faced.

They emerged from the dense jungle onto a narrow, rocky path that wound up a steep incline.

The path was treacherous, and the ground beneath their feet was loose and crumbling, forcing them to cling to the rock wall for support. As they ascended, the wind picked up, howling through the gaps in the rocks and sending chills down their spines. "Surely, this has to be the right way," Maya said.

Jake nodded, though he wasn't entirely sure himself. "The Keeper said the path would reveal itself. This must be it." The incline grew steeper and the path narrower until they reached a plateau that jutted into open space.

The view was both breathtaking and terrifying. Below them, the island spread out like a lush green carpet, the jungle stretching out to the distant beaches. But it was the sky above that caught Jake's attention.

Thick clouds swirled overhead, dark and menacing, their shapes twisting and turning like something alive. The wind intensified, tugging at their clothes and hair as if trying to pull them off the cliff's edge. Jake stepped closer to the edge, peering down into the abyss. It was impossible to see the bottom; the swirling mist obscured everything, creating the illusion of endless nothingness.

Maya stepped up beside him, clutching her jacket tightly around her. "This must be the place," she said, trembling. "But where's the bridge?" The clouds parted slightly in response to her question, revealing a structure suspended high above the ground. A narrow rope bridge stretched across the chasm, its ropes frayed and weathered, the wooden planks swaying precariously in the wind. The bridge seemed to lead directly into the clouds, disappearing into the thick mist on the other side.

Jake felt his stomach lurch at the sight. The bridge was impossibly high, suspended in a place where the line between the earth and the sky blurred. It was as if the bridge was suspended between two worlds, with the ground far below and the heavens just out of reach. The sight alone made his legs feel like jelly. "We have to cross that!?" Maya asked, shaking her head.

Jake nodded though every fibre of his being screamed at him to turn back. "The Keeper said the bridge was a riddle. I think... I think crossing it is the only way to solve it." Maya swallowed hard, "But what if we fall?" Jake forced himself to take a step closer to the bridge. "We won't fall. We can't let ourselves fall. We've made it this far, Maya. We must keep going."

With that, he took a deep breath and placed one foot on the first plank of the bridge. The wood creaked ominously under his weight, but it held. The wind whipped around him, tugging at his clothes and threatening to throw him off balance. Jake tightened his grip on the ropes and took another step and then another. Each step was a battle against the elements, the bridge swaying wildly with every movement.

Maya hesitated momentarily, then followed, her hands trembling as she grabbed the ropes. "I can't believe we're doing this," she muttered. The further they ventured onto the bridge, the more the wind seemed to pick up, as if the island itself was trying to stop them.

The clouds around them thickened, closing in and obscuring their view of the sky above and the ground below. It was as if they were walking into a void with nothing but the rickety bridge to guide them.

Suddenly, a loud creak echoed through the air, followed by a snap. One of the ropes holding the bridge in place began to unravel, sending the entire structure into a violent sway. Jake and Maya froze, their hearts pounding in their chests. The plank beneath Jake's foot wobbled dangerously, and he could feel the entire bridge beginning to tilt.

"Jake!" Maya cried out, her voice filled with terror. Jake gritted his teeth, forcing himself to stay calm.

"Don't look down! Just keep moving! You're doing a good job." He inched forward, each step more difficult than the last. The wind howled in his ears, and the clouds closed in around them, making it nearly impossible to see where they were going. But Jake knew they couldn't stop now. They had to reach the other side, no matter what.

As they moved deeper into the clouds, something strange began to happen. The mist around them started to change, taking on an almost tangible form. Jake blinked, trying to clear his vision, but the clouds seemed to coalesce into shapes—vague, indistinct forms that hovered just out of reach.

Maya gasped as one of the shapes moved closer, its edges solidifying into the unmistakable outline of an aeroplane. The plane appeared to be suspended in the mist, its body twisted and broken as if frozen in the moment of its crash. "It must be one of the aircraft lost here", Maya yelled over the howling wind.

Jake stared at the apparition, his mind struggling to process what he saw. "It's one of the lost planes. The ones that vanished in the Bermuda Triangle." As they continued to move forward, more shapes began to appear in the mist—ships, planes, even people, all seemingly trapped in the clouds, suspended between worlds. The wind carried faint whispers, the voices of those who had been lost, their words unintelligible but filled with despair.

The realization hit Jake like a punch to the gut. The bridge wasn't just a path across the chasm—it was a passage through time, through the very fabric of the Bermuda Triangle's mysteries. The riddle they had to solve wasn't just about crossing the bridge but about understanding the connection between the island and the disappearances.

As they neared the bridge's centre, the wind grew stronger, its force nearly lifting them off their feet. Jake tightened his grip on the ropes. The clouds around them swirled faster, the shapes within them becoming more defined, more real.

The air was thick with the smell of salt and smoke, the scent of the ocean mingling with the acrid stench of burning fuel.

"Look!" Maya pointed ahead. Jake squinted through the mist and saw a faint glow on the other side of the bridge, barely visible through the swirling clouds. It was the same light he had seen when he opened the box in the last challenge, a beacon guiding them forward. "We have to reach that light!" Jake shouted, his voice carrying over the wind.

They pushed forward, each step a battle against

the elements and the fear that threatened to paralyze them. The bridge creaked and groaned under their weight, the ropes straining against the wind's relentless assault. The shapes in the mist grew closer, their outlines sharper, as if they were reaching out to pull Jake and Maya into their eternal limbo.

Just as they were about to reach the glowing light, the bridge shuddered violently, and one of the planks splintered under Jake's foot. He cried out as he lost his balance, his body tilting dangerously toward the edge. For a moment, he was sure he would fall, plummeting into the abyss below. But Maya grabbed his arm, pulling him back onto the bridge with a strength born of sheer desperation. "We're almost there!" she shouted.

The wind howled around them, and the shapes in the mist reached out with ghostly hands, but they ignored it all and focused only on reaching the other side. Finally, they stepped onto solid ground, the light enveloping them in a warm, comforting glow. The wind died, and the mist dissipated, revealing the jungle beyond. They had made it.

Jake collapsed onto the ground, his entire body trembling with exhaustion and relief. Maya dropped beside him, breathing heavily, her eyes wide with disbelief. "We did it," she gasped, her voice filled with wonder and terror. Jake nodded, too drained to speak. The light that had guided them across the bridge was fading, but the sense of accomplishment and the knowledge that they had passed the Keeper's second test—remained.

But as the light dimmed, the Keeper's voice echoed through the clearing, a reminder that their journey was far from over. "You have crossed the bridge and faced your fear, but the truth remains hidden. The sky has spoken, and the path forward lies within the clouds." Jake's head snapped up, his eyes searching for the source of the voice, but the Keeper remained unseen. The mention of clouds scared Jake, reminding him of the visions they had encountered on the bridge.

"The clouds," Maya repeated, her voice trembling. "Does he mean we have to go higher?" The bridge had tested their resolve and ability to push through fear, but it was also a riddle—a puzzle that still needed solving. "What did he say earlier?" Jake asked, thinking back to the Keeper's earlier words. "Something about planes being lost in the clouds?" "Yes, he said the bridge was a riddle. And we saw those planes... those shapes in the mist."

Jake frowned, piecing together the puzzle. "The

Bermuda Triangle has always been associated with disappearances—planes and ships lost without a trace. But what if the clouds are the key? What if those who disappeared are somehow... trapped within them?" Maya's eyes widened as she realized what Jake was suggesting. "You think the planes we saw in the mist... they weren't just illusions, were they?" Jake shook his head slowly. "I don't think so. I think they were trapped in a place where time doesn't exist, where the rules of reality don't apply. And I think the next challenge is going to take us there."

Jake stood up, peering far above him. The clouds above were clearing, revealing a patch of blue sky that seemed almost surreal after the ordeal they had just endured. "We'll find the next piece of the puzzle," Jake said, his voice filled with resolve.

The Keeper's voice had faded, but its ominous message lingered in their minds. They had crossed the bridge and passed one trial, yet the island's mysteries remained unsolved. The thick clouds above still harboured secrets, and Jake realized their next trial would push them to their limits—and maybe even beyond.

CHAPTER 7

THE RIDDLE OF THE BRIDGE

Jake and Maya stood on the cliff's edge, staring up at the sky, where the last vestiges of the mysterious rope bridge faded into the mist. The air around them was still, almost eerily, as if the island was holding its breath, waiting for them to make the next move. Jake glanced at Maya, still catching her breath after their harrowing bridge crossing. She looked pale, fearing for her life.

"We have to go up," Jake said, breaking the silence. His voice sounded unnaturally loud in the stillness. "The Keeper said the path lies within the clouds. We need to climb higher." Maya agreed, though her eyes were wide and apprehensive. "But how? The cliff is too steep to climb, and we have no ropes or gear. It's like he expects us to fly."

The Keeper's challenges had tested their will and understanding, but they had also been puzzles that required them to think beyond the obvious. He looked around, searching for anything that might offer a clue when his eyes landed on a strange formation of rocks just a few feet away.

The rocks were arranged in a rough circle, and in the centre, there was a peculiar-looking stone pedestal, worn smooth by the elements but still distinctly out of place. Jake approached it cautiously, his heart pounding in his chest. The pedestal was covered in symbols—like those they had seen on the stone structure earlier—but these were different, more intricate and seemingly arranged in a pattern.

Maya followed closely, her curiosity piqued. "What do you think it is?" "I'm not sure," Jake replied, running his fingers over the symbols. The stone felt warm to the touch, almost as if it were alive. "But it looks like some kind of control or activation point." He pressed down on one of the symbols, and to his surprise, the stone pedestal began to glow softly.

The light spread across the symbols, illuminating them in a soft, ethereal blue. The air around them seemed to hum with energy, and Jake could feel a subtle vibration under his feet.

"This must be it," Maya said, her voice tinged with awe. "But what does it do?" As if in answer to her question, the ground beneath the pedestal began to tremble, and the circle of rocks slowly started to rise into the air. Jake and Maya stepped back in astonishment as the rocks lifted off the ground, hovering a few feet above the surface before slowly rotating around the pedestal. "It's like... a platform," Jake murmured, watching the rocks float effortlessly. "Maybe it's a way to reach the clouds."

Maya turned to Jake, "I think this will take us there!" "There's only one way to find out," Jake said, stepping onto the floating platform. The rocks held his weight effortlessly, and he felt a strange sensation of lightness as if gravity had lessened its hold on him. He extended a hand to Maya, who hesitated momentarily before joining him on the platform.

As soon as they were both aboard, the platform began to rise slowly, lifting them higher and higher into the sky. The ground below receded, and the jungle, the cliffs, and the treacherous rope bridge became distant memories as they ascended into the swirling mist.

After what felt like an eternity, the platform slowed its ascent and came to a gentle stop, suspended in the heart of the clouds. The mist was so thick that Jake could barely see more than a few feet in front of him. The air was heavy with moisture, and every breath felt like a struggle.

Jake squinted through the mist. The mist shifted and changed as they formed vague shapes and patterns. At first, they were just indistinct blobs, but gradually, they became more defined and noticeable. Jake's heart skipped a beat as he realized what he was seeing.

The shapes formed into humanoid figures— dozens of them, all surrounding the platform. The fog obscured their features, but their presence was undeniable. They were the lost souls of the Bermuda Triangle, the ones who had vanished without a trace. Maya gasped as one of the figures floated closer, its ethereal form barely visible through the mist. "Jake... what are they?"

"I think... I think they're the people who disappeared," Jake replied, his voice trembling. "The ones who were trapped here in the clouds." The figures moved closer, their movements slow and deliberate, as if drawn to the living beings in their midst. Jake could feel their eyes on him, even though he couldn't see their faces. There was a sadness in the air, a deep, profound sorrow that seemed to emanate from the very clouds themselves.

"They're lost," Maya whispered, her voice choked with emotion. "They've been trapped here for who knows how long... and they can't find their way out." The clouds were a prison where time and reality twisted and bent, trapping those who ventured too close to the Bermuda Triangle's mysteries. They couldn't leave these souls here, trapped in this eternal limbo. There had to be a way to free them, to break the cycle and finally end the Bermuda Triangle's curse.

"We have to help them," Jake said desperately. "We can't leave them here like this." "But how? How can we help them when we don't even know how to get out of here ourselves?" Maya replied quickly. The clouds were the key—he was sure of that.

They manifested the Bermuda Triangle's power, the force that trapped these souls in endless despair. But there had to be a way to break through, to shatter the illusion and set them free.

He reached into his pocket and pulled out the crystal they had found in the last challenge. It still glowed with a soft, ethereal light, pulsating gently in his hand. The crystal was connected to the island's power, and Jake felt it was the answer to their current predicament. "Maybe the crystal can help," he said, holding it up so that Maya could see. The crystal reflected brilliantly off Maya's eyes as she stared at it transfixed.

Maya suddenly snapped out of it, "I think this can break the connection. Free them from the clouds!" "It's worth a try," Jake replied, though he wasn't entirely sure. The crystal had already proven to be a powerful tool, and if it was connected to the island's energy, then perhaps it could disrupt the force that held the souls captive.

Taking a deep breath, Jake held the crystal before him, focusing on the spectral figures surrounding them. The crystal began to glow brighter, its light piercing through the fog and casting a soft blue hue over the entire platform. The figures hesitated as if sensing the change in the air.

The mist around them began to swirl and twist, and Jake could feel the energy in the air growing stronger. The crystal pulsed with light, and the clouds seemed to respond, their shapes shifting and bending in response to the crystal's power.

"Come on," Jake whispered, willing the crystal to work. "Break the connection. Set them free." The light from the crystal intensified, growing brighter and brighter until it was almost blinding. The mist roiled and churned, and the figures began to fade, their forms dissolving into the swirling clouds. Jake could feel the tension in the air, the very fabric of the clouds straining against the crystal's power.

And then, with a sudden burst of light, the crystal shattered the illusion. The mist exploded outward, the clouds dispersing in all directions and revealing the clear blue sky beyond. The spectral figures dissolved into the air, their forms breaking apart like wisps of smoke caught in a breeze.

Jake and Maya shielded their eyes from the blinding light, but when they looked again, the clouds were gone. The platform was still suspended in the air, but the sky was clear, and the weight of the mist had lifted.

Jake felt a wave of relief wash over him, though it was tinged with sadness. The souls were free but had also vanished, leaving nothing behind but the empty sky.

"We did it," Maya said softly, her voice filled with awe and sorrow. "We set them free." They had been trapped for so long, lost in the clouds, and now they were finally at peace. But the journey wasn't over— not yet. The Keeper's challenges were far from finished, and Jake knew the hardest trials were still to come.

As the platform descended, returning them to the ground below, Jake steeled himself for whatever lay ahead. The island had tested them in ways they could never have imagined, but they had survived and uncovered a truth that few others had ever glimpsed.

As they touched down on solid ground again, Jake glanced at Maya, looking out at the horizon with a determined expression. They were in this together and would see it through to the end.

CHAPTER 8

CRYSTAL CLEAR

Jake and Maya had barely caught their breath from the last trial when the ground beneath their feet started to shift again. The island, ever merciless, refused to grant them any respite. The sky above darkened as if a storm were gathering, and the rumble of thunder echoed ominously across the jungle canopy. The crystal in Jake's hand pulsed with a deep, almost frantic rhythm, reacting to the energy around them.

"Not again," Maya groaned, looking around frantically for the source of the disturbance. She had hoped—naively, it seemed—that they would have a moment of peace after surviving the horrors of the bridge. But the island was relentless.

"We have to move!" Jake shouted as the wind whipped against his face. Moisture hung in the air, almost like a warm tap sprayed over them. Without waiting for a reply, Jake grabbed Maya's hand and pulled her toward the edge of the clearing, where the jungle opened to a steep, rocky descent leading down to the coastline.

As they stumbled down the slope, the rumbling beneath them intensified, and the sound of crashing waves came with it. The path ahead of them suddenly gave way, the ground splitting apart as massive cracks raced toward the ocean, now visible through the thinning trees. The sea, usually calm and inviting, was churning violently like the very earth beneath it was rising and falling with each tremor.

Jake and Maya finally reached the bottom of the slope, where the jungle met the sandy shore. The ocean loomed before them, its waters an unnatural shade of green that shimmered with an eerie glow under the darkening sky. The waves crashed against the jagged rocks lined the beach, sending up sprays of saltwater that stung their skin.

"This doesn't feel right," Maya said, trembling. She gazed out at the ocean, where something dark and massive was moving beneath the surface. The shape was indistinct, but it was clear that whatever it was, it was enormous—and getting closer. Jake followed her gaze, his heart pounding in his chest. "We don't have a choice. Whatever the island is throwing at us, it's coming from out there." He pointed toward the water, where the dark shape was now circling, creating a whirlpool that sucked the surrounding water into its depths.

As they watched, the sea began to recede, pulling back from the shore and exposing the wet, sandy bottom. The retreat was swift and unnatural—like the ocean was being drained into a giant sinkhole. And then, without warning, the water rushed back with terrifying speed, crashing against the shore with the force of a tsunami.

Jake barely had time to react before the wave hit them. The water engulfed them, knocking them off their feet and dragging them into the depths. The force of the current was overwhelming, pulling them away from the shore and into the open ocean.

Jake struggled to keep his head above water, gasping for breath as the saltwater stung his eyes and filled his mouth. He reached out for Maya, who thrashed in the water beside him.

"Maya, hold on!" he shouted, though the ocean's roar drowned out his voice. He managed to grab her arm, pulling her close as they were swept further out to sea. The water was icy cold, and Jake could feel the strength draining from his limbs with each passing second. The crystal in his pocket pulsed weakly, its light dimming as if it, too, were being smothered by the water. The dark shape beneath the surface was closer now, its massive bulk casting a shadow over them.

Suddenly, the water around them began to churn violently, and Jake felt a powerful force pulling them downward. He tried to kick against it, but it was too strong. An unseen current dragged them into the depths, down toward the dark, cold abyss below. "Jake!" Maya screamed, her voice filled with terror. She clung to him desperately, her nails digging into his arm as they were pulled under the surface.

The last thing Jake saw before the darkness swallowed them was the distant, stormy sky rapidly receding above them.

The water closed in around them, cutting off all light and sound. Jake could barely see Maya in the inky blackness, though he could feel her trembling beside him, her grip on his arm tightening as they were pulled deeper into the abyss.

The pressure was intense, crushing them from all sides as they descended into the cold, silent depths of the ocean.

Just when it seemed they would be pulled down forever, the current suddenly stopped, leaving them floating in the still, icy water. Jake gasped for breath, his lungs burning from the exertion. He could feel his heart pounding in his chest, and the cold was so intense that his limbs felt like lead. He reached out for Maya, finding her hand in the darkness. "Are you okay?" he asked.

"I think so," Maya replied, her voice uneasy. "But where are we? What just happened?" "I don't know," Jake admitted. "But I think we're—" He stopped mid-sentence as something cold and smooth brushed against his leg. He froze, fear gripping him as he realized what it was. "Maya", he said slowly, his voice tight with fear. "Don't move. There's something down here with us."

Maya stiffened beside him, and Jake could feel her pulse quicken. "What is it?" she whispered, her voice scratchy. Before Jake could respond, the water around them began to move again, and he felt the cold, smooth skin brush against him again. This time, it was followed by a sharp tug, pulling him downward with incredible force.

Jake struggled to break free, but the grip was too strong. He was being dragged deeper into the abyss, away from Maya and the faint light of the crystal. The water around him churned violently as he was pulled downward, his lungs burning as he struggled to hold his breath.

He could barely make out the creature's shape in the darkness—long, sleek, and terrifyingly fast. It was a shark, and it was dragging him down to the depths. Jake kicked and thrashed, trying to free himself, but the shark's grip was unyielding.

Just as his vision began to blur from lack of oxygen, Jake felt a sudden surge of energy from the crystal in his pocket.

The light flared brightly, illuminating the water around him and causing the shark to release its grip in surprise. Jake seized the opportunity, kicking free and swimming upward with all his strength. He broke the surface with a gasp, gulping in air as he frantically looked around for Maya.

She was only a few feet away, struggling to stay afloat as the water churned around her. Jake swam to her, grabbing her arm and pulling her close.

"We have to get back to shore!" he shouted, his voice hoarse from the exertion. He could see the dark shapes of more sharks circling below them, their sleek bodies slicing through the water with terrifying speed. But there was no escape. The current was too strong, and the shore was too far away. They were trapped in the open ocean, surrounded by sharks and the endless, unforgiving water. Maya was shivering uncontrollably, her teeth chattering from the cold.

Jake looked around desperately, searching for any sign of hope. And then he saw it—a faint glow beneath the water's surface, growing brighter with each passing second. The crystal reacted to the danger around them, its light cutting through the darkness.

"We have to use the crystal!" Jake said. "It's the only way out of this!" Together, they held the crystal between them, focusing on the light as it grew brighter and brighter. The sharks circled closer, their movements frenzied as they sensed their prey.

And then, with a sudden burst of energy, the crystal flared to life, sending a shockwave of light and energy through the water. The sharks recoiled, their sleek bodies twisting in pain as the light seared through the water. The current shifted, pushing Jake and Maya upward, away from the sharks and the cold, dark depths below.

The light intensified, enveloping them in a warm, protective glow. Jake felt the pressure of the water lessen; the cold receded as the crystal's energy lifted them higher and higher, away from the dangers of the deep. And then, with a final burst of light, they broke through the surface, the crystal's energy propelling them onto a small, rocky outcropping that jutted out from the shoreline. They collapsed onto the rocks, gasping for breath and shivering from the cold.

The ocean around them was calm once more, the sharks nowhere in sight. The stormy sky had cleared, replaced by the soft, golden light of the setting sun. The crystal's light faded, leaving only a faint glow as it lay between them on the rocks. "We made it," Jake said, his voice hoarse with relief.

He looked over at Maya, who was lying beside him, her eyes closed as she caught her breath. "Yeah," she whispered, her voice trembling. "But how much longer can we keep this up?"

The island had tested them in ways they could never have imagined, and he knew there were still more challenges to come. But for now, they had survived, which was all that mattered. "We'll find a way," Jake said, unsure if he believed it.

He looked out at the ocean, which was now calm and peaceful as if the horrors of the deep had never existed.

The island had spared them—for now. But Jake

knew it was only a matter of time before it would strike again, with another challenge that would push them to their limits. He only hoped that when the time came, they would be ready.

CHAPTER 9

THE KEEPER'S WRATH

Jake and Maya trudged through the dense undergrowth, the jungle seemingly closing in with each step. The path ahead was barely visible, obscured by low-hanging branches and vines that seemed to reach out like ghostly fingers.

The sky above had darkened to a bruised shade of purple, casting an eerie glow over the landscape. The Keeper's lair lay deep within the island's heart.

"We're getting close," Jake whispered. The weight of the final crystal, warm in his pocket, gave him a strange sense of dread and hope. Maya's eyes fixed on the ground ahead as they continued their cautious advance. "I can feel it, too. It's like the island is alive, watching us, waiting."

The path finally opened into a wide clearing,

revealing the Keeper's lair—a massive stone temple half-sunken into the earth, its entrance flanked by two towering statues of ancient, faceless guardians. The stone was cracked and worn, covered in vines and moss, but the carvings on its surface glowed faintly with evil energy, pulsing in time with the rhythm of the island's heartbeat. Jake took a deep breath, readying himself. "This is it."

Together, they approached the entrance. The air grew colder with each step, and a deep, rumbling sound rang from within the temple, like the growl of some ancient beast awakening from a long slumber. They exchanged a glance—there was no turning back now.

Inside, the temple was dimly lit by flickering torches lining the walls, casting long shadows that danced and twisted like living things. The walls were lined with more carvings depicting scenes of ancient battles, lost civilizations, and sacrifices to appease the dark forces that governed the Bermuda Triangle. The floor beneath their feet was uneven, cracked, and littered with bones—human remains from those who had come before and failed.

At the temple's centre was a large, circular chamber, and in the middle stood the Keeper. He was more imposing than before, his figure no longer shrouded in shadow. The Keeper had shed his human-like form, revealing his true appearance: a towering, spectral figure draped in tattered robes that seemed to be woven from the very fabric of the night. His face was hidden beneath a hood, but his eyes—two orbs of burning, malevolent light—pierced through the darkness, locking Jake and Maya with an intensity that froze them.

"So, you've come at last," the Keeper's voice echoed through the chamber, deep and resonant, sending shivers down their spines. "To what end, I wonder? To claim the island's secrets for yourselves? To face your doom like all the others?"

"We're here to end this. The island, the disappearances, all of it. We're going to stop you," Jake yelled at the Keeper. The Keeper laughed, a sound that reverberated through the chamber like thunder.

"Stop me? You foolish children. You cannot stop what has been ordained since time immemorial. The island's power is eternal, and I am its guardian. You will share the fate of all those who came before you."

With a flick of his hand, the Keeper summoned a whirlwind of dark energy that filled the chamber, swirling around him like a storm. The ground beneath Jake and Maya's feet began to shake violently, cracks spreading across the stone floor as if the temple was coming alive, ready to swallow them whole. Jake reached into his pocket and pulled out the crystal, its light intensifying as it met the Keeper's dark energy. "We're not afraid of you," he shouted over the storm's roar. "This ends now!"

The Keeper hissed in response, raising both arms high into the air. The storm around him grew fiercer, the wind howling as it whipped through the chamber, tearing at Jake and Maya's clothes and forcing them to shield their eyes from the debris. The ancient relics lining the walls began to tremble, rattling against the stone like something terrible would be unleashed.

Then, with a deafening crack, the statues flanking the temple entrance shattered, and from the debris emerged two monstrous figures—gargantuan stone golems brought to life by the Keeper's will.

Their eyes glowed with the same malevolent light as the Keeper's, and they moved with a terrifying purpose, their footsteps shaking the very ground.

"Maya, watch out!" Jake yelled as one of the golems swung a massive arm toward her. Maya barely managed to dive out of the way, rolling across the ground as the golem's fist smashed into the spot where she had stood just moments before, pulverizing the stone floor.

She scrambled to her feet, her heart racing, and reached for the makeshift weapon she had fashioned from a piece of debris.

Jake, meanwhile, focused on the crystal, willing its power to activate. He had no idea how to use it, but he knew it was their only chance. As he gripped it tightly, the crystal began to glow even brighter, its light pushing back against the darkness.

The energy it emitted was warm and reassuring, like the first rays of sunlight after a long, cold night. The Keeper snarled, sensing the threat. "You cannot defeat me with that trinket, boy! The island's power flows through me, and I am invincible!"

Jake ignored him, concentrating harder, feeling the crystal's energy surge through him. Suddenly, the light from the crystal erupted in a blinding flash, filling the entire chamber. The golems froze in place, their movements halted by the light's power. The storm around the Keeper faltered, its dark energy struggling against the pure, unyielding light.

The Keeper roared in fury, summoning all his strength to push back against the light, but it was too late. Jake could feel the crystal drawing energy from the island, weakening the Keeper's hold over it. The temple walls began to tremble, the carvings glowing with a soft, blue light as if the island was responding to Jake's call.

"We have to focus, Jake!" Maya shouted, dodging another attack from one of the golems. "The crystal—it's draining the island's power! We're winning!" But the Keeper wasn't done yet. With a furious scream, he raised his arms once more, and the ground beneath them began to split open, revealing a chasm filled with writhing shadows. The temperature in the chamber plummeted as a cold, unnatural wind swept through the temple.

"You think you can defeat me?" the Keeper bellowed. "I will drag you into the depths of the abyss, and you will never see the light of day again!" The chasm began to widen, the shadows growing more solid, forming into clawed hands that reached out toward Jake and Maya.

The very air seemed to be sucked into the void, pulling them closer to the edge. Jake struggled to maintain his grip on the crystal, feeling the pull of the abyss, threatening to tear it from his hand.

"Jake, don't let go!" Maya screamed, her voice filled with panic as she clung to a piece of debris to keep from being dragged into the chasm. "I won't!" Jake shouted back; his voice strained with the effort. The light from the crystal began to flicker as the

Keeper's dark energy pushed back, and Jake felt his strength lessening. He couldn't hold on much longer—the island's power was too great, and the Keeper was relentless.

But then, during the chaos, Jake felt a presence—a comforting, familiar warmth that seemed to wrap around him like a protective shield. It was as if the island itself was reaching out to him, lending him its strength, urging him to keep fighting. "Jake... you have to believe!" a soft and reassuring voice whispered in his mind. The island wants to be free... you must believe in yourself!"

Jake closed his eyes, focusing on his warmth and connection with the island. The crystal responded, its light growing stronger, pushing back the darkness. The shadows recoiled, retreating into the chasm as the light filled the chamber once more. The Keeper howled in rage, his form flickering like a dying flame. "No! This cannot be! I am the island's guardian! I am eternal!"

Jake opened his eyes. "No... you're not. You're just a relic of the past. It's time for you to go." With one final push, Jake channelled all his strength into the crystal. The light burst forth, blinding and pure, filling every temple corner. The walls began to crack and crumble, the very foundations of the temple shaking as the island's power was released from the Keeper's control.

The golems disintegrated into dust, their forms collapsing under the weight of the light. The chasm in the ground sealed shut, the shadows vanishing as if they had never existed. The storm around the Keeper dissipated, leaving him standing alone, his form fading, becoming more transparent with each passing second.

"No…" the Keeper whispered, his voice filled with disbelief and fear. "This cannot be… I cannot be defeated…" Jake stepped forward, holding the crystal high. "It's over." The Keeper let out one final, anguished scream before his form dissolved completely, disappearing into the ether. The light from the crystal flared one last time, then slowly faded, leaving the chamber in silence.

Jake stood there, breathing heavily, his hand still clutching the now-dull crystal. He felt a wave of exhaustion wash over him but also a deep sense of relief. It was over. The Keeper was gone, and the island's power had been freed. Maya slowly got to her feet, her eyes wide with shock and disbelief. "Jake… you did it. You did it."

Jake smiled, his legs feeling weak beneath him. "We did it. Together." The temple around them continued to shake, the walls cracking and crumbling as the island's power was released. They had to get out before the entire structure collapsed. "Come on," Jake said, grabbing Maya's hand. "We have to move!"

They ran back through the temple, dodging falling debris and leaping over cracks in the floor as the entire structure began to cave in around them. The air was filled with the sound of stone grinding against stone, the ancient temple groaning as it finally succumbed to the forces that had held it together for centuries.

They burst out of the temple's entrance just as the entire structure collapsed behind them, sending dust and debris billowing into the air. The ground beneath them trembled, the island shifting and changing as if waking from a long, troubled sleep. Jake and Maya didn't stop running until they reached the edge of the jungle, where they finally collapsed, gasping for breath. The temple was gone, buried beneath tons of rubble, and the island was silent again.

For a long moment, neither of them spoke. They lay there, staring at the sky, trying to process everything. The Keeper was gone. The island was free. "We did it," Maya said again, her voice trembling. "We did it." Jake smiled, feeling a sense of peace settle over him. "Yeah... we did." The sky above them began to lighten, the dark clouds parting to reveal a clear, blue sky. The storm that had threatened to consume them was gone, replaced by a calm, serene atmosphere.

As they lay there, the first rays of sunlight broke through the clouds, bathing the island in a warm, golden light. It was as if the island thanked them, showing gratitude for freeing it from the Keeper's grasp.

Jake smiled, feeling the warmth of the sun on his face. They had survived the final battle. They had freed the island and all the souls trapped within it. And now, it was time to go home.

CHAPTER 10

THE ISLAND'S FAREWELL

Jake and Maya lay on the soft, warm sand of the beach, their chests rising and falling with the slow, deep breaths of exhaustion. The temple had collapsed, the Keeper was defeated, and the island had been freed from its ancient curse. The adrenaline that had fueled their desperate escape drifted away, leaving them both drained but deeply relieved.

Above them, the sky was a brilliant blue, the sun shining with a warmth that felt almost like a gentle embrace. The sounds of the jungle were distant now, replaced by the rhythmic crash of waves against the shore. For the first time in what felt like forever, Jake allowed himself to relax, closing his eyes and letting the sun's rays wash over him.

They lay there for a few moments longer, basking in the sun's warmth, the tension of the past hours slowly melting away. Once a place of darkness and fear, the island seemed almost peaceful, as if it was finally at rest. The nightmare was over.

But then, as they lay there, a shadow passed over them. Jake opened his eyes and saw a cloud drifting across the sun, casting the beach into an eerie, sudden gloom. The temperature dropped noticeably, and a cold wind began to stir, sending a shiver down his spine. Maya sat up, her eyes looking toward the horizon. "Jake... something's wrong."

Jake's heart sank as he saw the dark clouds gathering on the horizon. The peaceful moment was gone, replaced by a sudden sense of urgency. The island, which had seemed so still and serene just moments ago, now felt hostile again, as if the forces they had unleashed were not yet fully spent.

"We need to get off this island," Jake said. He scrambled to his feet, pulling Maya up with him. "If the island is collapsing, we can't stay here." They didn't need to say anything more. Together, they began to move quickly along the beach, searching for anything that could serve as a means of escape. The wind picked up, the once-gentle waves growing more violent as they crashed against the shore. The island's collapse had begun, and they knew they had little time.

The seemingly endless beach stretched before them with no sign of help. But then, as they rounded a bend, Jake spotted something that made his heart leap—a small lifeboat partially buried in the sand. It was old, weathered by the elements, but it was their only hope. "There!" Jake shouted, pointing to the boat. "We can use that!"

They sprinted toward the lifeboat, the sand shifting beneath their feet as they ran. The wind howled around them, the sky darkening with each passing second as the storm clouds rolled in. The peaceful beach was transforming into a scene of chaos, the island's final act of desperation.

Together, they reached the lifeboat and began to push it out of the sand, their muscles straining with the effort. The boat was heavier than it looked, its wooden frame creaking as they heaved it toward the water. But adrenaline and fear gave them strength, and soon they had the boat afloat, the waves lapping at its sides.

"Get in!" Jake urged, climbing into the boat and holding his hand to Maya. "We need to get as far from the island as possible!" Maya grabbed his hand

and climbed into the boat, quickly taking up the oars. The wind tugged at her hair, and the waves rocked the small boat as she began to row with all her strength. The island loomed behind them, a dark silhouette against the churning sky, its once-proud landscape crumbling into the sea.

Jake kept his eyes on the island as Maya rowed, watching as the jungle they had fought so hard to survive began to collapse in on itself. The ground split open, trees toppled like matchsticks, and the temple's ruins disappeared beneath the rising waves. The island was dying, and with it, the secrets of the Bermuda Triangle were being lost to the ocean's depths. "Keep going, Maya!" Jake shouted over the roar of the wind. "We're almost clear!"

Maya gritted her teeth, her arms burning with the effort, but she didn't slow down. They had to escape—they had come too far, survived too much, to be taken down now. The boat surged forward, riding the crest of a wave that carried them further from the shore. But the storm was growing stronger. The sky was almost black now, lightning flashing ominously in the distance. The wind howled around them, whipping the sea into a frenzy. Rain began to fall in heavy sheets, soaking them to the bone and making it nearly impossible to see.

"Wait... I think I see something! Out there—it looks like a ship!" Maya said excitedly. Jake squinted through the rain, his heart leaping with hope as he spotted a dark shape on the horizon. It was a ship—a large vessel cutting through the waves, its lights glowing like beacons in the storm. Help was within reach. "Row toward it! Hurry!" Jake yelled with joy. The ship was their only chance.

With each stroke, Maya put everything she had left into rowing, the lifeboat inching closer to the ship. The waves continued to batter them, but the ship was getting closer, its lights growing brighter as they approached. The storm raged around them, but Jake could see that they were almost there—almost safe.

Finally, they reached the ship's side, the lifeboat slamming into the hull with a jarring thud. A rope ladder was thrown over the side, and Jake grabbed it, his hands aching from the cold. "Climb up!" he shouted to Maya. "I'll hold the boat steady!" She grabbed the ladder and began to climb, her wet clothes clinging to her as she fought against the wind and rain. Jake held the boat steady, his hands trembling from the cold and exhaustion, as he waited for her to reach the deck.

When Maya was safely aboard, Jake followed,

climbing the ladder with the last of his strength. The wind howled around him, the rain blinding him as he struggled to pull himself up, but he didn't stop. He couldn't stop—not now. Finally, he reached the top, and strong hands grabbed hold of him, pulling him onto the deck. Jake collapsed, gasping for breath, as the ship's crew surrounded him, their voices filled with concern.

"Are you okay? Where did you come from?" one of the crew members yelled. Jake nodded weakly, too exhausted to answer. He could feel the ship's engine rumbling beneath him as it powered through the storm, carrying them away from the collapsing island. The danger was over. They were safe.

Maya knelt beside him, her face pale and drawn, but she managed a small smile. "We did it, Jake. We're safe now, I think." The ship's crew helped them to their feet, guiding them to the safety of the cabin. Inside, the warmth was a welcome relief from the cold, and Jake and Maya were quickly wrapped in blankets, their shivering bodies slowly beginning to relax. As they sat in the cabin, sipping hot drinks and trying to recover from their ordeal, Jake couldn't help but think about the island—how it had been their enemy, their greatest challenge, and yet, in the end, it had also been their ally. The island's collapse had freed them, just as they had freed it from the Keeper's control.

The storm outside slowly began to clear, the rain easing to a drizzle and the wind dying down. The ship sailed through the calm waters, carrying Jake and Maya away from the Bermuda Triangle and back to safety. They had seen things and done things that few others could ever understand. And while they had escaped the island, the memory of it would stay with them forever.

As they huddled together in the cabin, the ship's crew bustling around them, Jake reached into his pocket and pulled out the crystal. It was no longer glowing, its power spent, but it was still warm to the touch. He held it up, showing it to Maya. "This... this is the proof," Jake said softly. "The proof that it all happened."

"We'll never forget, Jake. We'll never forget," Maya replied. Jake slipped the crystal back into his pocket, leaning against the cabin's wall. The ordeal was over, but the adventure would stay with them for the rest of their lives. They had survived the Bermuda Triangle, faced its darkest secrets, and emerged victorious.

They had beaten the odds, escaped from the clutches of an ancient evil, and found their way back to the world they knew. But they also knew that the mysteries of the Bermuda Triangle were far from over. Somewhere out there, beyond the horizon, the secrets of the Triangle still waited, hidden in the ocean's depths, waiting for those brave enough—or foolish enough—to seek them out.

For now, though, they were content to leave those mysteries behind, return home with their story and memories, and live their lives knowing they had faced the darkness and won.

CHAPTER 11

UNFINISHED BUSINESS

The sky above the Miami airport was a perfect blue, and the world felt warm and alive as Jake and Maya stepped off the plane and back into reality. After everything they had endured, the ordinary sounds of people chattering, luggage wheels clicking on the smooth floor, and the announcement of delayed flights were comforting, almost surreal. It was as though the island and all its mysteries were a world away, buried beneath the sea and its dark secrets.

Jake took a deep breath, filling his lungs with the familiar air of home. It felt strange to be back as if the adventure they had survived had somehow changed the air he was breathing. Maya walked beside him, quiet but alert, her eyes scanning the busy airport terminal. Neither had spoken much since the ship rescued them and brought them back to Nassau. They had barely slept, their minds too tangled with thoughts of the island's collapse and what they had witnessed.

But now, everything felt distant back in Miami— almost like a dream. Jake wasn't sure if he should be relieved or disturbed by how quickly life moved on. People bustled around them, unaware of what Jake and Maya had been through. To everyone else, it was just a normal day. "Feels weird, doesn't it?" Maya broke the silence as they walked toward the exit. "Being back... here, in the real world."

"Yeah. We've been gone forever, but everything's still the same here. Like nothing changed," he replied. Maya smiled, though there was a hint of sadness in it. "Except us." They stepped out into the warm, humid air of Miami. Jake's mom was waiting for them near the curb, her face breaking into a broad grin as soon as she spotted them. "Jake! Maya!" she called, waving enthusiastically. She ran toward them, pulling Jake into a tight hug before doing the same to Maya.

"You two are a sight for sore eyes," she said, her voice shaky with relief. "When I heard about the storm and then that you two had been missing for days... I thought—" She stopped herself, wiping a tear from the corner of her eye. "I'm just so glad you're safe." Jake returned her hug, a lump forming in his throat. "We're okay, Mom. We're fine, and we're back now."

As they drove back to Jake's house, the city buzzed with the familiar sights and sounds of everyday life. Cars honked in the distance, children played in the park, and the world seemed so... normal. Jake and Maya exchanged glances, silently acknowledging that they had left something far more extraordinary behind.

When they reached Jake's house, his mom fussed over them, ensuring they had food, drinks, and anything else they might need. She hovered, asking questions about their trip—about the "boring" contest details, the flight, and the Bahamas. They gave her answers, but only the ones that made sense. They didn't tell her about the storm, the temple, or the Keeper. Some things were too strange to explain, and they knew no one would believe them anyway.

After an hour or so, Maya glanced at her phone and stood up from the couch. "I should probably get home," she said, giving Jake a quick smile. "My parents are probably freaking out too." Jake nodded.

"Yeah, you're probably right. We'll talk later?" "Definitely," Maya replied quickly, grabbing her bag. "You think... it's really over?" Jake's hand instinctively moved to his pocket, dull and silent, where the crystal now rested. "Yeah," he said softly. "I think it is." Jake's mum shot them both a weird look.

Maya gave him a small smile before heading out the door. Jake watched her go, then leaned back against the doorframe, feeling a strange mix of relief and uncertainty. It wasn't until later that night after his mom had gone to bed, that Jake finally allowed himself to sit in his room and really think about everything. He pulled the crystal from his pocket and placed it on his desk.

The once vibrant light that had pulsed through it was gone, and now it looked like nothing more than a piece of polished stone.

But Jake knew better. He had seen what it was capable of—what it represented. The crystal had been at the centre of everything. It had led them to the island, to the Keeper, and had ultimately helped them defeat him. Now, it was just... there. A reminder of the adventure they had survived and the secrets that still lurked in the Bermuda Triangle.

Jake stared at it for a long time, trying to make

sense of the whirlwind of emotions swirling inside him. Part of him felt he should be grateful to be alive and home. But another part of him couldn't shake the feeling that the adventure wasn't over. The island might be gone, but something about the crystal still felt... alive.

He stood up and crossed the room, pulling open his closet. In the back, hidden beneath some old clothes and forgotten toys, was an old wooden box. It was once used for baseball cards but would now serve a different purpose.

Jake opened it and carefully placed the crystal inside, tucking it away where it couldn't be seen. The crystal was hidden now, with all the island's mysteries—at least, that's what he told himself.

The next few days passed in a blur of normalcy. Jake returned to school, slipping back into his routine of classes, homework, and hanging out with his friends. But there was an underlying strangeness to everything. He zoned out in class, his mind wandering back to the island, the temple, and the Keeper.

Sometimes, he would catch Maya's eye across the classroom, and she would give him a knowing look as if she, too, was struggling to adjust.

People asked about their trip—about the

Bahamas and the contest. Jake and Maya kept their answers vague, sticking to the script they had agreed on: they had flown to the Bahamas and spent some time exploring but had gotten caught in a bad storm that delayed their return. It wasn't the most exciting story, but it kept people from asking too many questions.

For the most part, life went back to normal. But now and then, Jake would catch himself staring out the window, wondering if the island had sunk beneath the ocean. Or if, somehow, its power still lingered, waiting for the right moment to resurface.

It wasn't until the following weekend that things took an unexpected turn. It was a quiet Saturday morning, and Jake had slept in for the first time in weeks.

The sunlight streamed through his window, casting long, lazy shadows across his room. He stretched, yawning as he sat up in bed, his mind still groggy from sleep. That's when he noticed it.

The crystal he had hidden away in the wooden box at the back of his closet was glowing. At first, Jake thought he was imagining it. He rubbed his eyes, blinking against the sunlight, but the glow was unmistakable. It was faint, a soft, pulsing light, but it was there—the same light he had seen on the island just before everything had fallen apart.

Jake got out of bed and crossed the room. He opened the closet, his hands trembling slightly, and pulled out the wooden box. His breath caught in his throat as he lifted the lid.

The crystal was glowing. Not as brightly as before, but enough to make the hairs on the back of his neck stand up. "What the..." Jake muttered under his breath. He stared at the crystal, unsure of what to do. Hadn't its power been spent? Hadn't the island's collapse ended whatever hold it had over the crystal?

Before he could think any further, his phone buzzed on the desk. It was a text from Maya.

Maya: Dude... you need to check your crystal.

Jake's stomach did a flip. He quickly typed a response. Before Maya left, he decided to split the crystals up, so gave Maya another one.

Jake: Wait, is yours glowing too?

There was a long pause before the dots appeared, signaling Maya was typing. His heart pounded in the silence, every second stretching like an eternity.

Maya: Yeah. It started this morning. What's going on?

Jake glanced back at the crystal, the faint pulsing light reflecting off the box's surface. Something was happening. Something they hadn't accounted for. Without waiting for another text, Jake dialed Maya's number. She picked up after the first ring. "Jake, what's happening? Why is the crystal glowing again?" Her voice was shaky, on the edge of panic. "I don't know," Jake said, staring at the glowing stone. "I thought we stopped this. We freed the island, right?"

"That's what we thought," Maya replied. "But... if the crystal's still active... maybe we didn't finish everything. Maybe there's something we missed." Jake sat on the edge of his bed, trying to steady his thoughts.

"What if the crystal's trying to tell us something? What if we didn't destroy the Keeper completely?" Maya was silent for a moment, considering his words. "You mean... he could still be out there?"

Jake ran a hand through his hair, his mind racing. "I don't know. But whatever this is, it's not over." Maya sighed on the other end of the line. "What do we do now, Jake? Should we tell someone?" Jake stared at the crystal, the soft glow filling the room with an eerie light.

The thought of returning to the mysteries they had tried so hard to leave behind made him nervous. But deep down, he knew they couldn't ignore this.

The island might be gone, but its power wasn't finished with them yet.

"We're going to have to figure it out," Jake said, his voice steady despite the fear in his chest. "We're going to have to go back."

The End

www.ingramcontent.com/pod-product-compliance
Lightning Source LLC
Chambersburg PA
CBHW070406200726
48294CB00003B/1125